T0129278

THE CASE OF THE
MISSING
POLICE HORSE

Wendy Elmer

authorHOUSE®

AuthorHouse™
1663 Liberty Drive
Bloomington, IN 47403
www.authorhouse.com
Phone: 1-800-839-8640

Published by AuthorHouse 1/11/2013

ISBN: 978-1-4817-0605-6 (sc)
ISBN: 978-1-4817-0606-3 (e)

CHAPTER 1

Mordecai Dunne was an ex con who couldn't get a job. He couldn't get unemployment because of being an ex con.. He was essentially homeless because nobody would rent to him. He had to make a plan to change this. He lied on his application by using his brother's name. He got the apartment, but was evicted a month later because he got caught. He didn't think the landlord would actually check into the information. He missed being in jail only because he had shelter and three square meals a day. He figured that he just had to pretend to be suicidal. That got him into isolation. In the middle of the night he came up with the perfect plan. IT was a minor crime, but it brought him time to make something of his life. He called his old friend and cell mate Mitchell Dubey. Mitchell was told to meet him in the diner at 10:00 the following morning. They met and ordered breakfast.

CHAPTER 2

After the waitress took their orders Mitchell said: "So Mordecai. What can I do for you?"

Mordecai said: "I was let out of jail and have been essentially homeless ever since. People won't rent to me because I have a police record. I can't get a job because of my police record. When I was in jail they put me into a small box and didn't give me any life skills to survive on the outside. In school all they taught me was academics, not life skills. They didn't teach me about speaking like an adult."

Mitchell said: "They always said if you can't do the time don't do the crime."

Mordecai said: "That is no excuse for not preparing me for life. The educational school system stinks. It's no wonder we turn to a life of crime."

Mitchell said: "If you don't like the school system just start a letter writing campaign and show up at school board meetings. That would be more productive than just whining about how everybody else screwed up your life except you. You seem to think everyone else screwed up your life."

Mordecai slapped his face hard right there in the diner. Mitchell had blood running out of his mouth. The waitress offered to call the cops, but Mitchell waved him off.

Mordecai said: "I have a plan to get back into jail but for a minor crime."

Mitchell asked: "Wait a minute. Before you do anything rash have you talked to your parole officer about your difficulties? He is required to help you get a job and a place to live. He needs to step up to the plate and do his job. I think you can request a new parole officer if you are unhappy with the one you have."

Mordecai said: "Do you think I can just stroll into a police station with my record?"

Mitchell said: "Why not? The worst they can tell you is to tell you to go back to the warden and talk it over."

Mordecai slapped his face again on the other side. Mitchell said: "This is really getting old. Your slapping me like that just doesn't work anymore."

At this point the manager of the diner threw them both out.

CHAPTER 3

The next day they continued their conversation. Mitchell said: "So brainiac. What is this master grand plan you have?"

Mordecai said: "We are going to steal a police horse." Mitchell threw a glass of water in his face. He said: "Then what abandon it in the middle of the woods?"

Mordecai said: "Naturally. What a brilliant plan you have. I knew I could count on you."

Mitchell said: " Here's another brilliant plan. Leave the horse unattended in the middle of the night on the strip. At 3:00 in the morning the only people out are the prostitutes."

Mordecai said: " I have a better plan than that. I want $100.000.00 for ransom for the horse."

Mitchell said: "What have you been drinking? If you steal a police horse you will be guaranteed a return trip to jail. That is a major felony messing around with police equipment. How do you plan to pull it off anyway?"

Mordecai said: "You are going to help me. On June 14th is flag day. Everybody will be at the parade. We sneak into the police headquarters and steal one."

Mitchell said: "In the first place getting anywhere near there is worse than getting into Fort Knox. Unless you have a police uniform on you aren't getting past the front gate. I already checked it out. I walked up there and pretended to be a tourist. He let me in and gave me a glass of water. I told him I was a bit overwhelmed by the heat. I wasn't prepared for it. There was a guard right inside the door. All the horses were standing up with the snout hanging over the edge of the stalls. I couldn't get close to any of them because I was told to sit right next to the cop. I did as I was told."

Mordecai asked: "How long did they let you stay?"

Mitchell said: " They let me stay just long enough to get a glass of water. I wiped my face down and then left. I thanked him for his hospitality."

Mordecai asked: "Was there a special patch they wore to show they were from the mounted police unit?"

Mitchell said: "No. All they had was a pin that said LVMPD and a real gun on the waist band. I am unsure if they wore a stun gun or not."

Mordecai said: "You did good. You just made a plan for me to follow. Go home now until I call for you."

Mitchell went home and made a phone call to Mordecai's parole officer. He also took up the issue with his own parole officer. He wanted to warn them of the impending event. He wanted to warn the cops also, but his parole officer told him not to say anything to anyone. He didn't feel good about it, but went along with it anyway.

He was trying to be a model parolee.

CHAPTER 4

On June 13th Mitchell received a phone call from Mordecai about pulling off this caper. Mordecai instructed Mitchell to meet him at his house at 11:00 that evening. He was given a police uniform and a pin that said LVMPD on the collar. He was told to put it on and come out of the bathroom within 5 minutes. He didn't have all night. He was given a gun belt and a 45 caliber pistol. It looked like a police gun at first glance. Luckily the handle was the same. He came out and was dragging his feet all evening. He was given a police shield, but it was fake because it was a silver shield and not a gold one. They broke into the horse stables at midnight. Mordecai saw the cop and gave him a nose full of formalgehyde. It knocked him out right away. They got past the guard by karate kicking the guard at the booth. While the inside guard was in dreamland Mitchell grabbed the first horse he saw and led them away. Mordecai was impressed with this move. He didn't think Mitchell knew anything about horses. They made it outside and rode away. Down the road they stopped long enough to talk about what to do with it. Mordecai was so smart he forgot to think that far ahead. They decided to bring it into the woods for the evening. They slept with it the first night. In the morning they woke with a fresh new look at the day. Mitchell mentioned that he was surprised that the other horses didn't make a big runkus over the intrusion. Mordecai went out for breakfast and came back again. Mitchell went out to get a pail of water from the creek for the horse. The only thing he knew that horses ate was carrots. He forgot those too. Now they were stuck in broad daylight and not place to hide a horse or feed it anything. Mitchell had to leave because he had an appointment with a parole officer. At first Mordecai said not to go, but nothing was going to keep Mitchell from his appointments.

The rest of the team pulled him back down into h seat.

Schapiro said: "Take a chill pill John. We all know how you feel about horses. Screaming at me doesn't get the horse found. Now let's break down and analyze the situation."

Peter asked: "Where was the horse last seen?"

Schapiro said: "He was last seen at the stables."

John said: "Wait a minute. I was the last one to ride him yesterday."

Schapiro said: "That is why we were called in to solve this case. Go over with me everything you can recall about yesterday. You know I am talking about the horse, so don't start out with your breakfast."

John said: "We were having a good day. I put him to bed after our shift and left him. Nothing exciting happened to upset either one of us. We walked along the strip and the families wanted to take his picture. He is a ham. He smiled for the camera. A few kids wanted to sit on him. I let them do it and helped them up and down off of him. When we got back to the stables I fed him and watered him and left him for the day. Our usual routine was very uneventful. I don't know what else to say."

Schapiro said: "Okay John. If you think of any thing or anyone at all just speak up."

CHAPTER 5

Meanwhile back at the stables the morning guard came in and found his predecessor on the ground still knocked out cold. He called for an ambulance and he accompanied him to the hospital. He woke up in the ambulance feeling dizzy and woozy. He was able to tell the cop he was karate kicked in the head. Then it was lights out. The sergeant is going to want a full report. The paramedics said he was going to be okay. He was admitted to the hospital overnight for observation. He came back to work a week later.

The guard on the inside wasn't so lucky. He got a nose full of formalgehyde and woke up and couldn't remember a thing. He was out on disability for a month. When he was finally able to put a story together he gave it to the sergeant. He remembered getting a nose full of rag, but couldn't name the contents of what was on it. He had to be told what was on it. He suffered a lot of headaches for a long time after that. The first question he asked about was the horses.

The sergeant said: "There was one horse stolen. He is still missing. It was the one named Commissioner."

The guard said: "There is only one horse finder who can take on this case. It was Detective Schapiro."

The sergeant said: "Everybody knows who that is. Commissioner was involved in that case of the missing child just about 2 years ago. He was ridden by a new member of the team named John. I will make that call right now."

CHAPTER 6

Detective Schapiro was in his office whe phone jangled in his ear. He spilled his fee all over himself as usual. He prom to get right on the case as soon as he called his together. They were there within 5 minutes of ting the call.

He said: "Praise God we have a case. Somet stole a police horse last night. John, do you rem ber that horse you rode two years ago into St. Pe Church?"

John said: "Yes sir. He was a beautiful ho Nice and gentle."

Detective Schapiro said: "That's the one that stolen."

John nearly crawled over the desk and grab Schapiro by the collar. He almost had to be strained. He screamed out: "If anyone touches hair on that horse's mane I will shoot him mysel

CHAPTER 5

Meanwhile back at the stables the morning guard came in and found his predecessor on the ground still knocked out cold. He called for an ambulance and he accompanied him to the hospital. He woke up in the ambulance feeling dizzy and woozy. He was able to tell the cop he was karate kicked in the head. Then it was lights out. The sergeant is going to want a full report. The paramedics said he was going to be okay. He was admitted to the hospital overnight for observation. He came back to work a week later.

The guard on the inside wasn't so lucky. He got a nose full of formalgehyde and woke up and couldn't remember a thing. He was out on disability for a month. When he was finally able to put a story together he gave it to the sergeant. He remembered getting a nose full of rag, but couldn't name the contents of what was on it. He had to be told what was on it. He suffered a lot of headaches for a long time after that. The first question he asked about was the horses.

The sergeant said: "There was one horse stolen. He is still missing. It was the one named Commissioner."

The guard said: "There is only one horse finder who can take on this case. It was Detective Schapiro."

The sergeant said: "Everybody knows who that is. Commissioner was involved in that case of the missing child just about 2 years ago. He was ridden by a new member of the team named John. I will make that call right now."

CHAPTER 6

Detective Schapiro was in his office when the phone jangled in his ear. He spilled his coffee all over himself as usual. He promised to get right on the case as soon as he called his team together. They were there within 5 minutes of getting the call.

He said: "Praise God we have a case. Somebody stole a police horse last night. John, do you remember that horse you rode two years ago into St. Peter's Church?"

John said: "Yes sir. He was a beautiful horse. Nice and gentle."

Detective Schapiro said: "That's the one that was stolen."

John nearly crawled over the desk and grabbed Schapiro by the collar. He almost had to be restrained. He screamed out: "If anyone touches one hair on that horse's mane I will shoot him myself!!"

The rest of the team pulled him back down into his seat.

Schapiro said: "Take a chill pill John. We all know how you feel about horses. Screaming at me doesn't get the horse found. Now let's break down and analyze the situation."

Peter asked: "Where was the horse last seen?"

Schapiro said: "He was last seen at the stables."

John said: "Wait a minute. I was the last one to ride him yesterday."

Schapiro said: "That is why we were called in to solve this case. Go over with me everything you can recall about yesterday. You know I am talking about the horse, so don't start out with your breakfast."

John said: "We were having a good day. I put him to bed after our shift and left him. Nothing exciting happened to upset either one of us. We walked along the strip and the families wanted to take his picture. He is a ham. He smiled for the camera. A few kids wanted to sit on him. I let them do it and helped them up and down off of him. When we got back to the stables I fed him and watered him and left him for the day. Our usual routine was very uneventful. I don't know what else to say."

Schapiro said: "Okay John. If you think of anything or anyone at all just speak up."

John asked: "What happens if we never find the horse?"

Schapiro said: "I don't know. Let's worry about that in the future. In the meantime go home for the day. I will talk to the commissioner about it. Since you are personally involved you are forbidden to work on the case."

John left the precinct feeling rather dejected. This just ruined his whole week. He felt helpless just sitting on his hands not doing anything. He managed to obey Schapiro's orders not to get involved in the investigation.

CHAPTER 7

The commissioner's name was Norman Johnson. He requested an audience with Schapiro and John. Detective Schapiro called John the next day and requested that he show up at 10:00 to the precinct. After the three of them met in Schapiro's office they adjourned to the interview room for suspects. Schapiro came in with three cups of coffee and a plate of chocolate chip cookies. Schapiro knew this would make John relax a little.

Norman said: "Good morning John. My name is Normal Johnson. You have no need to be afraid of me. The only reason we are here is to figure out what happened. I am only human just the same as you. If you get nervous just picture me sitting here in my underwear. How scary can that be?"

Schapiro spit his coffee out through his teeth with laughter. John also did that trying to picture his boss in his underwear. He mentioned just for laughs that he has always been a boxers kind of guy.

Norman said: "Let us begin this interview. How long have you been a cop?"

John said: "About three years now."

Norman asked: "How did you get on the mounted police squad?"

John said: "I excelled in all my classes at the academy. The higher ups believed I should be a mounted cop. I only had one screw up in training. The first time I mounted a police horse I was facing the tail instead of the snout. It took the commanders twenty minutes to stop laughing. Even the horse was making laughing sounds. They told me it was called whinnying when a horse does it."

Norman asked: "What made you want to become a cop to begin with?"

John said: "I had just gotten out of jail about a month previous to that. I met Schapiro in the supermarket and he encouraged me to take the exam. I passed on the first try. Everybody he spoke to said I would be a good choice."

Norman asked: "When you got out of jail what made you decide to settle in Las Vegas?"

John said: "I was in jail and had information about a murder. It turned out he was lying, but he was found out anyway and the real killer was executed. The real killer was his twin brother. I became a model prisoner and never got into trouble again. I talked to psychiatrists in jail and he helped me get my life on the right path. Schapiro entered my life and we have been working with each other ever since. I still moonlight at the Motel 6 motel as a handyman. I do that on the weekends."

Norman asked: "How long have you been working with this particular horse?"

John said: "About a year now. I first started working with him on a missing child case. The horse heard St. Peter's Church and he took off like a rocket. I couldn't control him for beans. He stood right in front of the altar and refused to move an inch. I just let the horse catch his breath. Schapiro came out an almost dirtied himself with shock. The pastor came out and started making goo-goo noises and tickling the horse on his chin. The horse and I have been inseparable ever since."

Norman asked: "When you brought the borse back to the stables did you see anything out of character?"

John said: "No sir. I saw the guard at the outside gate and dismounted. I walked him to his first stall and cleaned him off. I took the brush and pail and cool water and rubbed him down. I took his saddle off and hung it up. I fed him and gave him fresh water. Then we parted for the evening."

Norman asked: "Did you close and latch the door locked securely?"

John said: "Yes sir. I always double check the lock just to make sure."

Norman said: "Okay John. That will be all for now. Report to the precinct tomorrow morning for your regular shift. Schapiro will have filing for you to do. We are giving you a break from street patrol for a while."

John said: "Okay sir. But what will happen if we never find the horse?"

Norman said: "My gut feeling is that we will. I think it was college pranksters. Perhaps a fraternity initiation. Don't even think about that worst case scenario. Please go home now. Schapiro will walk you to the front door. Keep you head held up high and don't slouch."

CHAPTER 8

When they left the room Schapiro told John to do exactly as Norman said. When Schapiro returned to the office Norman asked: "Does he always look that green around the gills?"

Schapiro said: "He has a very strong emotional attachment to that horse. He feels guilty about the whole situation."

Norman asked: "Do you have confidence that he will follow my instructions to the letter?"

Schapiro said: "Absolutely sir. No question about it."

Norman said: "Since he is directly involved he is not allowed to get involved in the investigation for any reason. Is that clear?"

Schapiro said: "Yes sir. Chrystal clear."

Norman said: "Now I have an assignment for you. Clean up your office. Have John help you tomorrow if necessary. I don't tolerate sloppiness from my detectives."

Schapiro said: "Yes sir. I will get to work on it right away."

They departed company for the day. Schapiro looked around and tried to figure out where to start. He gave up and went home for the day. He called John later in the day just to make sure he got home safely. John sounded depressed, but at least he got home okay. Schapiro told him to just watch TV and eat a healthy lunch and dinner. Things will always look better in the morning. Maybe an idea will pop into his head at the most unexpected time. Usually when you are asleep you will come up with something. They hung up and John went back to bed.

CHAPTER 9

In the middle of the night Mitchell couldn't handle it anymore. He took the horse and abandoned it in the middle of the strip. Mordecai will want his head on a platter, but he didn't care. He was tired of his company and trying to pull him down the wrong path. Mitchell was lucky that Mordecai left him alone with the horse. He could finally make his move. Mitchell led the horse to a lake and the horse drank from it. Then the two of them walked out and onto the strip. He was abandoned on Freemont Street, which is the busiest place to be. He was led into the inside mall and left there. Mitchell felt vindicated to be rid of it. He just walked away like any other tourist pulling an all nighter.

John in the meantime couldn't sleep for beans. He finally got up and went out for a walk. He knew his instructions from the commissioner, but he didn't know what to do. He called Schapiro's house. His wife answered on the third ring. Schapiro didn't move a muscle. He was too zonked out. He always slept like the dead.

His wife said sleepily: "Hello?"

John said: "Good morning Mrs. Schapiro. My name is John. I work with your husband Robert. I am on his squad. He told me to call him anytime day or night. I was hoping I could talk to him."

Mrs. Schapiro said: "I'll see if I can wake him. He sleeps rather deeply you know."

John said: "Thank you Mrs. Schapiro. Robert got on the phone a few minutes later. His wife was surprised that he got up on the first shake. He must have been awake already.

Robert got on the phone and said: "What's wrong son?"

John said: "Sorry to wake you sir. But I couldn't sleep. I can't focus enough for sleep to come. I don't know what to do about this horse thing.

Robert said: "Do you remember your instructions? You are not allowed to get involved in the investigation. You have work in a few hours. I don't want to see bags under your eyes tomorrow."

John said: "Okay sir. Sorry to disturb you."

Robert got back into bed and his wife said: "What's wrong with John tonight?"

Robert said: "Didn't I tell you? Somebody stole

the horse John has been riding for a year now. They are like two peas in a pod. He feels guilty for it. It happened in the middle of the night. The commissioner won't allow him to partake in the investigation. He is beside himself. I told him to get some sleep. The most I could tell him was that I didn't want to see bags under his eyes tomorrow morning."

Mrs. Schapiro asked: "Do you think he will do as you tell him?"

Robert said: "If I tell him not to take a leak for twenty four hours that idiot will hold it in that long." They bade each other good night and went back to sleep.

CHAPTER 10

John went out for a walk and wandered aimlessly about the streets. He showed up for work at 9:00 the next day. Schapiro took one look at him and asked if he had slept at all.

John said: "No. I stayed up and watched Law and Order. Then it was time to come here."

Schapiro said: "Go home for the day. You are in no shape to do any filing. I will talk to the commissioner myself. Don't worry about him."

At that point the commissioner walked into the office. He took one look at John and asked: "How much sleep did you get last night?"

John said: "None at all."

Norman said: "Please go home John. You are in no shape to be here today. I won't even dock you for the day. I know you are worried about the horse, but your not sleeping isn't doing any good. Schapiro will drive you home."

John said: "Yes sir. I will do as you ask."

Schapiro did as he was asked to do. When they got to John's house Robert reiterated the instructions not to get involved with the investigation. John went upstairs and flopped into bed. He was out like a light in five minutes. He woke up at 11:00 that night. He decided to take a walk on Freemont Street. There were stores there that were open 24 hours a day. Looking at that stuff always seemed to relax him. He got a sight of it and almost fell over with excitement. He at first thought he was dreaming. But then Commissioner the Horse started neighing at him. They knew each other the minute they saw each other. They nuzzled and hugged each other. John had to figure out a way to get the horse out of the inside mall. He didn't want to chance either of them getting stuck through the revolving doors. John picked up his cell phone and dialed Schapiro's phone number at home. The answering machine came on and he screamed into it "I FOUND COMMISSIONER!!!"

Schapiro jumped up and picked up the phone. He screamed back "WHAT ARE YOU TALKING ABOUT?"

John screamed: "THE HORSE!!! I found him in the inside mall on Freemont Street!!"

Schapiro said: "Stay with the horse. Don't either of you move. I will call the authorities and get you safely out of there. Schapiro hung up the phone and an hour later the proper authorities showed up outside the mall. Norman showed up for the show also. They walked through the swinging doors. John was standing there with the biggest possible grin on his face and declared "Here he is!! I found my horse!!"

Norman said: "Congratulations John. You just recovered police equipment. Now tell me one thing son. How are we going to get the horse out of here?"

John said: "Through the doors. I gather he wasn't lowered from an airplane from the roof."

Schapiro asked: "Does a horse fit through the swinging doors?"

John said: "Gee. I don't know. So that's why you're all standing around scratching your heads in wonderment. I'll bet I can get him through the swinging doors He will do anything for me. Let me try."

Schapiro relented and said: "Fine John. Let's see what idea you come up with. John whispered sweet nothings into the horse's ear. He had to relax him first.

Schapiro said: "If you get that horse through

the doors I will personally write a $100.00 donation to the local animal shelter. The real commissioner said: "I will double that. Let's see what you can do." They both ate their words because both the horse and John made it through the revolving doors. They both through a temper tantrum right there in the mall. People stopped and stared at the show. Everybody wanted in on the action. By the end of the hour the animal shelter got a donation of $2,000.00. Nobody believed it possible.

Norman said: "Alright John. I will never doubt you again. Escort the horse back to the stables and report to Schapiro's office tomorrow morning at 9:00. We will now start the investigation part of this scenario. Stay with the horse until he is settled in, fed, watered, and brushed. Then go home and get a good night's sleep."

John said: "Yes sir. Absolutely."

CHAPTER 11

During the day Norman did an interview with Matthew, the guard at the gate. He finally felt well enough to at least work with a sketch artist. They came up with a sketch of two people. These sketches were handed over to Schapiro and his team. Schapiro and his team took the sketches to police uniform stores. They hit pay dirt on the second try. Matthew remembered seeing one fellow previously. He spun a tail of being a tourist overcome with the heat. He stayed long enough for some water. He was then escorted out of the stables. Schapiro took the sketches to his old friend Mary Kelly, the warden of the prison in California. He was looking for a possible name on these two characters. Mary recognized them right away. Mordecai Dunne and his friend Mitchell Dubey. She asked: "What did they do now?"

Schapiro said: "They stole a police horse by the name of Commissioner."

Mary said: "That I believe is a major felony. Touching police equipment. If I were to venture a guess Mordecai would be the person to look at. Mitchell was just a tag along."

Schapiro said: "Thanks Mary. That helps a lot."

As soon as Schapiro got back to the office he put an APB out on these two suspects. Mitchell turned himself in the next day and Mordecai was apprehended at a homeless shelter. He was apprehended with violence. He kicked and punched the officers and it took eight people to hold him down. When he arrived at the police station he had to be seated in a restraint chair. When he finally shut up the nurse took his blood pressure. It was 220/180. That was really bad news.

CHAPTER 12

Mitchell was led into an interrogation room. He was given a cup of coffee and some cookies. The questioning was done by Schapiro himself. His first statement was: "You are not under arrest at this time. That is why we don't have to read you your rights. You do not need a lawyer at this time. You have a right to request one at any time. You have ta right to leave at any time. Do we understand each other?"

Mitchell said: "Yes sir. I understand completely."

Schapiro asked: "Are you aware that this interview is being recorded?"

Mitchell said: "Yes sir. I have agreed to that."

Schapiro said: "Good. Let us begin then. How did you first meet Mordecai?"

Mitchell said: "We were cellmates in jail."

Schapiro asked: "Did you two get along?"

Mitchell said: "I tried to get along with him. We

just had to give each other space and we were fine with each other."

Schapiro asked: "Did he respect the rules of the jail?"

Mitchell said: "Not really. He gave the guards a hard time. He was put in isolation a few times. I enjoyed that because I got the cell to myself for a while."

Detective Schapiro asked: "What rules specifically did he not cooperate with?"

Mitchell said: "It was the cell searches. He refused to leave the cell when told to."

Detective Schapiro asked: "How did the guards treat you specifically?"

Mitchell said: "During our orientation we were told we had two choices. We could follow the rules and life would be easy or we could not follow the rules and life would be difficult. I chose to follow the rules and try to get through my year in one piece. I had more privileges than Mordecai because I tried to cooperate. Luckily the warden allowed me to talk to a psychiatrist. I talked to him and he helped me to organize my life."

Detective Schapiro asked: "What were you in jail for?"

Mitchell said; "Simple robbery. Not even armed

robbery. I was the driver, but my friends didn't tell me they didn't pay for it. The cops pulled me over and everybody scattered. I willingly walked back to the store and that is when I learned what they did. The cops wrote it up and said I fully cooperated. The judge gave me one year in jail. I gave the cops the names, addresses, and phone numbers of al the gang. They each got five years. Really all I did was to fall in with the wrong crowd."

Detective Schapiro asked: "When the rest of your gang got to jail how did they treat you?"

Mitchell said: "They were kept in a separate building, so they never saw me."

Detective Schapiro said: "That will be all for today Mitchell. Report to your probation officer at your regularly scheduled time."

Mitchell said: "Uh. I think I should tell you something. He complained about not finding a job or an apartment. I told him to talk to his parole officer. Mordecai expressed anger over being himeless. He wanted to do a minor crime just to have three meals and a roof over his head."

Detective Schapiro said: "Okay Mitchell. The officer will show you out."

CHAPTER 13

The next day it was decided to take both of them into custody. Mitchell was picked up at his parole officer's office. He went with the cops without incident. The parole officer told Mitchell what to do. Finding Mordecai turned out to be a little more challenging. A cop noticed him shoplifting from a convenience store. He was arrested on the spot. When he got to the precinct he was recognized as a wanted man. He was transported to jail a few hours later. Schapiro was notified by phone of the latest event. Schapiro told them to hold him until morning. The judge ordered Mordecai to be held without bail. Mitchell was released on his own recognizance, which simply means he promised to show up for trial when told to. Mitchell went about his usual routine until he was told to show up for court. He was notified by his parole officer when to show up for court. He dressed appropriately and showed up punctually.

When Mordecai got to the jail he was booked and processed same as before. He gave the officers a hard time with the strip search. He was thrown into a cell with three other guys. He sat on his bed quietly and sulked away most of the night. The next morning he came around and started accepting his fate. At least he had shelter and three square meals for a while anyway.

CHAPTER 14

Jury selection started on Monday June 1st. It only took one day because it was a nonviolent type of case. The case was heard by Judge Mario Schwartz. He was glad to hear a nonviolent case for a change. He had been a judge for over thirty years. He had lived through death threats over cases he heard.

The morning of the first day of trial judge Schwartz made a last minute change. He decided to hear the two cases separately. This crime involved two different people. He heard the case of Mitchell first. He ordered Mordecai be returned to jail until the start of his trial date. He will be notified of his trial date through the warden. He explained that this means all the witnesses will be called twice. This made it easier to find one person guilty or innocent or both guilty. After Mordecai left the room jury selections began. They were finished with it by the afternoon. It started out badly because one person was a horse lover nad wanted nothing less than to shoot him at high noon in the middle of Times Square. She was dismissed right away. Everybody else seemed to want to be in on this case. With jury duty if you are dismissed you run the risk of being called for a worse case. Nobody wanted that.

CHAPTER 15

Mitchell's lawyer's name was Julian Martin. The prosecutor's name was Jack O'Malley. Secretly he also wanted to shoot him in the middle of Times Square. He had no choice but to put his personal feelings aside and do his best at his job. Just before the judge entered the court room for the day the bailiff yelled: "ALL RISE!!" Everybody rose and waited for the judge to be seated.

The judge said: "You may be seated."

Judge Schwartz opened the morning's festivities with the same lecture he gives all his cases. He said: "I am a no nonsense type of judge. I will tolerte no outbursts of anger from anybody. All parties in this case will conduct themselves in a professional manner. You will dress properly. Jury members will not wear shorts or talk during the proceedings. This case will be finished within five days." Even the bailiff and court officers stood at attention in his court room. He wouldn't tolerate so much as a sneeze out of turn. All of these rules seemed absurd or impossible to follow, but as a result he moved the court calendar fastest. The judge said: "Jack, you may begin with your opening statement."

Jack said: "Thank you judge. Ladies and gentlemen of the jury. This is a case of petty theft, but the price of the horse makes it a felony. You could find him guilty, but that doesn't mean he did it. The testimony will show that he did not actually touch the horse. He is only guilty by association . You must find him not guilty. Thank you."

The judge said: "Julian, please makte your opening statements."

Julian said: "Thank you your honor. Ladies and gentlement of the jury. We have a case her of somebody who got involved with somebody who was a bad person. His criminal record made him do this. The real guilty parties here is the jail system and the school system that failed my client. Thank you."

The judge said: "Jack, you may call your first witness."

Jack said: "I call Norman to the stand." As Norman approached he was sworn in as a witness. He said: "Please tell us Norman your occupation."

Norman said: "I am the police commissioner, also known as the chief of detectives, or chief of D's.

They are all the same thing. I am one person with three different titles."

Jack asked: "How did you get involved in this case?"

Norman said: "I was notified of the theft of the horse. It is considered police equipment, so I have to do the investigation."

Jack asked: "What were your actions when you learned of this?"

Norman said: "I received a phone call in my office. I then made a phone call to Detective Schapiro. He has a member on his team by the name of John."

Jack asked: "What was John's reaction to the news of the horse?"

Norman said: "You will have to ask Detective Schapiro. I was not a personal witness to his reaction."

Jack said: "Tell me about when you found the horse."

Norman said: "I never found the horse, it was John. When I got there John was standing there with the biggest grin on his face. I asked him how he was going to get the horse out of the building. He said he could get it out through the revolving door. I told him if he does that Robert will personally write a check to the animal shelter. I promised him Robert would make a donation of $100.00 and I would double it to two hundred dollars. By the time the hour was up we raised $2,000.00 in pledges. Everybody wanted in on the action. Sure enough he got that horse through the revolving door. I threw the mother load of all temper tantrums right there in public. Robert was breathless in shock at my behavior. Everybody was. I normally don't act like that."

Jack said: "Thank you. No more questions."

The judge said: "Julian, do you have any questions for this witness?"

Julian said: "Thank you your honor. Norman, did you interview the defendant?"

Norman said: "Yes. I was hiding out on the other side of the one way mirror. I was a witness to his questioning."

Julian asked: "Did he ever admit to stealing a horse?"

Norman said: "No. He never said he did it. He pointed the finger at Mordecai. He told us the whole sordid story."

Julian asked: "What was his role in the crime?"

Norman said: "He admitted to putting the horse through the revolving doors of the mall. He doesn't remember how he did it."

Julian said: "Thank you Norman. No more questions your honor."

The judge said: "You may step down Norman. Jack, call your next witness please."

Jack said: "I call Harry McCann to the stand. As Harry approached the stand he was sworn in as the witness. Jack said: "State your name for the record."

Harry said: "My name is Harry McCann."

Jack asked: "Do you remember the night the horse was stolen?"

Harry said: "I remember the event, but I don't remember when it happened."

Jack said: "Please tell us what exactly happened on that day."

Harry said: "I was the guard on the front gate. All horses and cops have to be buzzed in by me. The horses exit the trucks and are led in through the gates. I was just sitting there when I heard a knock on the window. I came outside and I was karate kicked in the head. Then it was lights out. I woke up dizzy and woozy in the ambulance. I returned to work a week later."

Jack asked: "Do you still feel the effects of that karate kick?"

Harry said: "Yes. But the police medical exam

showed I was fine for duty. I just had to promise to get checked out if I start to feel dizzy, forgetful, or light headed in any way. Then I was given clearance to go back to work."

Jack asked: "Are you on modified light duty for now?"

Harry said: "No. They would take my gun away from me if I were. I am back doing the same thing."

Jack said: "Thank you Harry. No more questions your honor."

The judge said: "Julian, do you have any questions for this witness?"

Julian said: "I do your honor. Harry, didn't you tell us you got out of your booth?"

Harry said: "Yes. I did. I heard a knock on my window, so I got out to see what this stranger wanted from me."

Julian said: "So, you broke the cardinal rule of guarding the horses. You turned your back on them didn't you?"

Harry said: "I never thought of it like that. I just thought of it as this stranger is lost and it is my duty to turn him around. We get a lot of tourists who want to see a police horse and where they live. The horse stables are off limits to tourists because they need a quiet place of sanctuary."

Julian asked: "Do you remember the karate kick to the head?"

Harry said: "Barely. It took me a while to get my senses back. I woke up in the ambulance and then again at the hosptial. I looked in the next bed and found my partner Mark. Nobody would tell me anything about him."

Julian asked: "Have you spoken to Mark since that night?"

Harry said: "I have spoken to him on the phone. He seems distant and disconnected. I paid him a visit to his house, but his wife wouldn't let me see him. The sergeant said he doesn't think he is coming back at all."

Julian said: "Thank you Harrry. No more questions your honor."

The judge said: "You make step down Harry. Jack, call your next witness please."

Jack said: "I call Mark McKinney to the stand."

Mark approached the stand very slowly. He waved his arms around to catch his balance.

The judge asked: "Mark, are you okay?"

Mark said: "Yes sir. Just a little shaky today."

The judge said: "Jack, support him and make

sure he doesn't fall." Jack helped him the rest of the way up to the stand and poured him a glass of water.

The judge said: "Jack will begin as soon as you are ready."

Mark said: "I am ready now sir. Thank you sir."

Jack asked: Do you remember the night of the horse being stolen?"

Mark said: "Vaguely. I get snatches now and then. I remember being on duty that night."

Jack asked: "What was written in your job description?"

Mark said: "I was supposed to make sure there are no intruders bothering the horses."

Jack asked: "Do you remember seeing the defendant as an intruder?"

Mark said: "I remember sitting in the chair and something on a rag on my face. Then it was lights out."

Jack asked: "Will you be going back to work?"

Mark said: "No sir. I am out on permanent disability."

Jack asked: "When was it that Detective Schapiro interviewed you?"

Mark said: "I don't remember. I can't tell time

anymore. Last week feels the same as yesterday. I need to rephrase that. I can tell time, but distinguishing time is all fuzzy to me."

Jack said: "Thank you Mark. No more questions your honor."

The judge said: "Because of the time we are adjourned until tomorrow morning at 9:00 a.m. Everybody be in your seats by then and ready to begin. In the jury assembly room they take attendnace at 9:30. I will pass down a note with your names on it and you will be marked as present. Have a good evening everyone." With that everybody left the building. Before the judge left the bailiff yelled: "ALL RISE!!" Everybody rose and then the judge left. They were then escorted out of the building by the bailiff. The judge left the bench for the day.

CHAPTER 16

The next morning right before the judge entered the courtroom the bailiff yelled: "ALL RISE!!!" The judge entered right at 9:00 and found everybody present just as instructed. He smiled and said good morning to the jury. It started his day on the right foot. He said: "Julian, you may call your first witness please."

Julian said: "I call Detective Schapiro to the stand." Detective Schapiro stood and approached the stand. He was sworn in as a witness. The bailiff said: "State your full name for the record please."

Detective Schapiro sadi: "My name is Robert Schapiro."

Julian asked: "How long was this police horse missing?"

Detective Schapiro said: "He was missing for approximately 48 hours."

Julian asked: "Was there a ransome demand?"

Detective Schapiro said: "No sir. Nobody called and demanded money for the horse."

Julian asked: "How did you find the horse?"

Detective Schapiro said: "It was my team member John who found him. John couldn't sleep so he went out wandering around. He found himself on freemont Street and looked in the window of the mall. There was Commissioner just standing there. John called me right away and I mobilized the teams to get down there right away. All the guys took care of John and the horse until the real Commissioner could get there. John is like the son I never had. We keep him safe because he is literally alone in the world."

Julian asked: "What did you find when you got there?"

Detective Schapiro said: "I found John with a big grin on his face from ear to ear. His face could literally not split apart any further or it would split in half."

Julian asked; "How did you get the horse through the revolving door?"

Detective Schapiro said: "John has a special bond with the horse. He has a gift that will never be duplicated by anyone else. If he told the horse to do cartwheels he would figure out what that meant and do it."

Julian said: "Thank you Detective Schapiro. No more questions your honor."

The judge said: "Jack, do you have any questions for this witness?"

Jack said: "I do your honor. New Detective Schapiro, how did you happen upon my client and accuse him of this heinous act?"

Detective Schapiro said: "The two guardds worked with a sketch artist. We took the sketch to the stors that sell police equipment and got lucky on the second try. Then we went to the county jail to see if the warden remembers anybody that looked like that. Sure enough we had a name. She also gave us the name of his cell mate. They were in on this together."

Jack asked: "Did you find my client's fingerprints on the horse or bridle?"

Detective Schapiro said: "No sir."

Jack asked: "Were the two officers disciplined?"

Detective Schapiro said: "No. They didn't do anything wrong. One tried to chase away a potential intruder and the other one didn't stand a chance. The one guard with a nose full of rag didn't know what happened. He is out on permanent disability so we can't discipline him anyway."

Jack said: "Thank you Detective Schapiro. No more questions your honor."

The judge said: "You may step down Detective Schapiro. Due to the time we will adjourn for the day. Everybody return here tomorrow morning by 9:00 a.m. We are dismissed. Good day everybody."

The bailiff yelled: "ALL RISE!!!" The jury was escorted to the front doors of the courthouse.

CHAPTER 17

Outside the court room John asked Detective Schapiro how he managed to get to court by 9:00 a.m.

Detective Schapiro said: "That is one judge you don't mess with. I am afraid to fart in his court room. I have to make sure I get to court on time. I have never gotten to know him as a person. I am sure he smiles sometimes. You must remember to answer only the questions the attorneys ask when you are on the stand. That judge tends to stare right through you."

John asked: "What do we do now that you are finished in court?"

Detective Schapiro said: "We return to the precinct to check out for the night. You can go home and play with your cat. It will make you feel better."

CHAPTER 18

Just before the judge entered the court room on day three of the trial the bailiff yelled: 'ALL RISE!!!" Everybody knew that was the clue that he was on the way in.

They were used to the routine by now. The day started at 9:00 just as expected. The judge entered and said: "Good morning to everyone. He said: "Julian, call your first witness please."

Julian said: "I call John to the stand."

As John approached he was sworn in as a witness. He was so nervous he tripped on the step going up to the chair.

The judge asked: "John, is this your first time testifying in court?"

John said: "No sir. I have done this about two times before."

The judge said: "There is no reason to be nervous. Just answer the questions the best you can. Tell the truth and don't worry about the outcome. Is it true you hurtled last time you testified?"

John said: "Yes sir. But at least I made it to the bathroom."

The judge said: "Julian, you may begin."

Julian asked: "How exactly did you get that horse through the revolving door?"

John said: "The horse and I have a special bond. He will do anything I tell him to do. I spent an hour whispering sweet nothings into his ear. We just played together and when he was ready, he went."

Julian asked: "How long was the horse missing?"

John said: "He was missing for about 48 hours."

Julian asked: "What was your reaction to the news of the horse's disappearance?"

John said: "I crawled across the desk and grabbed Schapiro by the lapels. I insisted that he find the horse personally. The other two team members pulled me back into my seat. After I calmed down Schapiro told me to not get involved in the investigation at all. I was instructed to return to the office the next day for an interview with Commissioner Norman. I was sent home for the day. Schapiro told me to try and relax until then."

Julian asked: "How did your interview with Norman go?"

John said: "Norman was a nice gentleman who told me to relax nad just tell the story."

Julian asked: "What did hyou do to get through this?"

John said: "Actually I couldn't sleep for two nights. I was worried sick about the horse. I tried to find comfort in my cat. He slept with me and knew something was amiss with me. We snuggled together, but it didn't work. I went out for a walk."

Julian said: "No more questions your honor."

The judge said: "Jack, do you have any questions for this witness?"

Jack said: "No questions your honor."

The judge said: "You may step down John." He then addressed the jury and said: "We will break for lunch now. Everybody return here in one hour and you will then be given instructions on your deliberations."

The bailiff yelled: "ALL RISE!!!" Everybody rose and left the courtroom for a well deserved lunch.

After lunch everybody returned to the courtroom for closing arguments. The judge said: "Julian, you may begin when ready."

Julian got up and said: "Thank you your honr. Ladies and gentlemen of the jury. The evidence speaks for itself. They were seen on tape buying cop uniforms. The defendant is obviously guilty of stealing the horse. His presence at the crime scene has been verified by at least three people. You must find the defendant guilty of stealing the horse."

The judge said: "Jack, you may begin when ready."

Jack said: "Thank you your honor. Ladies and gentlemen of the jury. You may have noticed that my client did not take the stand. That is because he already pled guilty to the charges. If he wasn't under the influence of Mordecai he would not have done this. You must find my client guilty of conspiracy to commit a felony, which causes a sentence of one to five years."

The judge was very appreciative of the short closing statements. He dismissed the jury for the evening and instructed them to sleep on the facts overnight. They were to return no later than 9:00 the next morning and be prepared to start deliberations. He bid them all fair well and left the cortroom. The bailiff yelled "ALL RISE!!!" Everybody rose and was escorted out of the building.

CHAPTER 19

The next morning everybody showed up on time. The judge said: "Good morning ladies and gentlement of the jury. I trust you have slept well last night. This moring you are to consider all the evidence and decide if the defendant is guilty or not. Take your time and don't rush through this dicision. You must use a note and pass it through the bae bailiff to communicate with me. Nobody is to leave that room until a decision has been made. There is a bathroom in the room. I have provided coffee and snacks for you to nibble on. Your first task is to appoint a foreman or forewoman. The job of that person is to hand me the note and then read it to me. It makes no difference who the foreperson is. I will go to you and dismiss you for lunch" With that last statrement the bailiff led them into the jury room. It was a simple room with windows to look out of. Juror number four volunteered to be the foreman. Everybody agreed to that. They took about a half hour to settle down and start talking about the case. There was a dispute over why the defendant didn't take the stand. Everybody had their own explanation for that one.

The bailiff had to remind them to shut up and start negotiating. They were all in agreement that he was guilty of conspiracy to commit a felony. The second part was to decide on the punishment. Some wanted to send him to jail and others wanted to send him to work with the homeless. The final decision was a compromise. The judge led the group back into the courtroom. The jury tok their seats. The defendant and his lawyer were not there, so they showed up a little later unaware that the jury had come to a conclusion. The judge dismissed them for lunch. Afte rlunch a very grouchy judge took attendnace. The defendant and his lawyer were in attendance. The judge said: "Has the jury reached a verdict?"

The jury foreperson said: "We have your honor. The note was passed to the judge. He said: "Will the defendant please rise?"

The jury foreperson said: We the jury find the defendant guilty of conspiracy to commit a felony. For his punishment we want the defendant to go around to the high schools and grammar schools and lecture them on the dangers of getting involved with the wrong crowd. He is also to visit the teen detention center and talk to them about this same subject."

The judge asked: "Do you understand your assignment?"

The defendant said: "Yes sir. I do understand. Thank you sir."

The judge said: "Bailiff, please dismiss the jury." The jury returned to the jury assembly room for dismissal.

CHAPTER 20

The jail was notified that Mordecai's trial will start on July 17th. Picking a jury was fairly easy this time around. There was no harm done to any humans. The jury was notified that the defendant will be returned to jail everyday during the trial, so they won't be followed home. Mordecai was confident he was going to get off scott free after this caper. Judge Schwartz was the judge for his trial. His lawyer was Julian. The prosecuting attorney was Jack. Same characters as in the first trial. The jury had no knowledge of the results of the previous trial because there was a gag order and the media was not informed of the previous trial. The judge assured the jury that their names and pictures will never be released to the media. Judge Schwartz opened the procedings by introducing himself and the lawyers to the jury. The jury was instructed to return by 9:00 a.m. the next morning. The lawyers were instructed to be prepared to begin opening statements. Lateness will not be tolerated. The jury was so nervous nobody wanted to challenge him on that one. The bailiff yelled "ALL RISE!!!" Everybody rose and left the courtroom.

CHAPTER 21

Day 1 of the trial started at 9:00 a.m. with the judge entering the courtroom. The bailiff yelled "ALL RISE!!"" That was the hint that the judge was on the way in. The jury would hear this twice a day for the duration of the trial.

The judge said: "Julian, you may begin with your opening statements now."

Julian said: "Thank you your honor. Ladies and gentlemen of the jury. My client pled guilty of stealing the horse. He had a good reason to do that. You will learn the reason during the course of this trial. He really meant no harm to the horse. There is no dispute that he karate kicked the guard. It was his partner that put the scheme into place. There is also no dispute that he gave the guard a nose full of rag. He also had a good reason to do it. You will find this out during the course of the trial. Thank you."

The judge said: "Jack, you may begin with your opening statements."

Jack said: "I am the prosecuting attorney. There will not be too much physical evidence to sift through. This trial will be more testimony than anything else. Feel free to take notes. The horse's bridle could not be brought in because he doesn't have a spare. He needs it to work everyday. Thank you."

CHAPTER 22

The judge apologized to the jury, but he had no choice but to dismiss the jury for the day. He got a text message that his wife was having a baby. She just went into labor. He requested that everybody return tomorrow morning at 9:00 He promised no m,ore interruptions. The jury all smiled at his anxiousness and bid him a good luck for the day. With that the bailiff yelled "ALL RISE!!" The jury was dismissed by the bailiff for the day. They were escorted out of the courthouse. The purpose of being escorted was just in case the elevator malfunctioned. Sure enough the elevator got stuck between floors and the bailiff had to take steps to get them out. He pushed the call button and help was sent. It took so long that he had to call on the walkie talkie to make sure somebody was on the way. The repair people were out on another job, so that is why it took so long. The job of the bailiff was to keep everybody calm and cool and collected. One poor soul lost control and panicked. She started sweating bullets and she wet herself. The bailiff had to call on the walkie talkie a second time and announce that there was a diabetic in the elevator. She was taken away in an ambulance for medical observation. Everybody else went home.

CHAPTER 23

Day two of the trial started at 9:00 a.m. with the bailiff screaming "ALL RISE"!!!! Everybody rose and the judge entered the courtoom with a huge smile on his face. He announced that his wife had a baby boy. They named him Mario Elijah, after him. His brisk will take place next Tuesday, so this trial will end before that. Now without further adieu we will begin with this trial. Jack, call your first witness please."

Jack said: "I call Sandy to the stand."

As Sandy approached the stand she was sworn in by the bailiff. Jack asked: "Do you know the defendant?"

Sandy said: "I waited on him at the diner I work at."

Jack asked: "By the way Sandy. Please tell us your full name."

Sandy said: "My name is Sandy Brown."

The judge interrupted and said: "Excuse me Sandy. Is this your first time on the witness stand?"

Sandy said: "Yes sir. I have never done this before."

The judge said: "Don't worry about anything. Just tell the truth and you will do fine. Please continue Jack."

Jack asked: "What kind of person is the defendant?"

Sandy said: "From what I could tell he has a very aggressive personality."

Jack asked: "Can you give us an example of his aggressive nature?"

Sandy said: "Yes. One day he came in with a friend and they were talking. All of a sudden he hauled off and slapped his friend across the face. That is when the manager threw them both out. We don't need that kind of behvior in our restaurant. We have other customers to consider."

Jack said: "No more questions your honor."

The judge said: "Julian, do you have any questions for this witness?"

Julian said: "I do your honor. Now Sandy, do you know what my client was talking about with his friend?"

Sandy said: "Technically I wasn't listening, so I don't know."

Julian asked; "For all you know they could have been talking about the weather."

Sandy said: "I couldn't care less what they were talking about. When they get that aggressive with each other there is no call for it."

Julian asked: "How long have you been waiting on the defendant?"

Sandy said: "Maybe about a year now. Sometimes he comes in alone and sometimes with a friend. Different people."

Julian asked: "Is he a good tipper?"

Sandy said: "Not really. He gives me a dollar, but I don't think he really wants to."

Julain asked: "Have you ever had the occasion to over hear any of his conversations?"

Sandy said: "Yes. I overheard him talk to his friend about the school system. I was running around that day, so I couldn't say exactly what was said. Every time I went to his table they both dummied up."

Julian said: "Thank you Sandy. No more questions for this witness your honor."

The judge said: "You may step down Sandy. Jack, call your next witness please."

Jack said: "I call John to the stand." As John approached he was sworn in by the bailiff. He managed not to trip on the step this time. He sat down and waited for Jack to begin. He was dressed in a 3 piece suit just like Schapiro told him to.

Jack said: "Good mroning John. You look much more relaxed than last time."

John smiled and said: "Thank you sir. I have had tutoring in this area and I am no longer as nervous as before."

Jack asked: Who has been tutoring you John?"

John said: "My boss Detective Schapiro and the Commissioner Himself. I am starting to get used to doing this."

Jack asked: "How were you involved in this case?"

John said: "We were notified because Commissioner the horse and I have been working together for about two years now. I am responsible for the horse's well being, care, and his life is in my hands. We have a special bond that can never be broken."

Jack asked; "What did you do when ou found out that your horse had been stolen?"

John said; "I went totally crazy. I crawled up on the desk and grabbed Schapiro by the lapels and demanded that he personally return the horse. After

I calmed down we were in a better position to talk it over. The next day I met Commissioner Norman in person for the first time. He was more excited about meeting me than anything else. He could tell how nervous I was. He just said I should picture him sitting there in his underwear. How scary is that? He believed me that I never wanted to hurt the horse. He also banned me from getting personally involved in the investigation. Schapiro put his foot down on that one. That was the difficult part. I managed to obey orders, so I went out for a walk in the middle of the night. Then I found the horse just standing there. It looked like he was waiting for me to take him home."

Jack asked; "What did you do then?"

John said: "I called Schapiro on the phone and told him the update. He told me to stay put and he will be right there. Within 5 minutes half the police force wa soutside the door. The wagon for transporting the horse arrived and then the boss showed up. All the guys wanted to say hello to the horse and pay their respects to him. Even the Commissioner wanted a ring side seat for this circus."

Jack said: "Thank you John. No more questions your honor."

The judge said: "Julian do you have any questions for this witness?"

Julian said: "Yes your honor. John, didn't you say the Commissioner barred you from the investigation?"

John said: "Yes sir. He did. Schapiro made it clear that Norman's instructions were to be followed to the letter."

Julian asked: "Then why were you out in the middle of the night looking for it?"

John said: "I wasn't looking for it. I was so upset I couldn't sleep, so I went out for a walk."

Julian said: "Thank you John. No more questions your honor."

The judge said: "You may step down John. Jack, call your next witness please."

Jack said: "I call Detective Schapiro to the stand. As Detective Schapiro approached he was sworn in by the bailiff. He then took his seat."

Jack asked; "How did you get involved with the case?"

Detective Schapiro said: "Whenever a new case comes up I am assigned by the sergeants to solve it. My team goes out and works the case until it is solved."

Jack asked: "Why you and not another detective?"

Detective Schapiro said: "This case involved a police horse. Everybody knows John is on my team. Everybody knows it was John's horse and everybody knows John was the last person to see the horse the day before. It was only logical that we get this assignment."

Jack asked: What was John's reaction to the news of the horse's disappearance?"

Detective Schapiro said: "He crawled on top of my desk and grabbed me by the lapels. He demanded that I personally return the horse back where he left it. We started the investigation soon afterwards. We just took it one step at a time."

Jack asked; "Did you disciplien him for disobeying orders?"

Detective Schapiro said: "He never disobeyed orders. He told me and Norman that he couldn't sleep. We both believed him. He gave me the same story he gave Norman on two separate occassions. He has never lied to us before and it is not in his nature to start lying."

Jack said: "Thank you Detective Schapiro. No more questions for this witness."

The judge said: "Julian, do you have any questions for this witness?"

Julian said; "Yes Your honow. Now Detective Schapiro, how did you come about blaming my client for this heinous act?"

Detective Schapiro said; "We did an interview with the cops that were effected by this event. They were both interviewed separately and both came up with the same sketch. We then took that sketch to the stores that sell police equipment. If someone loses their walkie talkie or if they need a new gun belt. They must show ID that they are indeed a cop. The second one we went to your client was identified as a customer. We then brought the sketch to the jail and the warden recognized both of them immediately. That is how we got their names. An APB was put out on both of them. His partner turned himself in. He told us who is parole fofficer was and when his appointment was. He practically handed him to us on a platter."

Julian asked: "Was he cooperative during questioning?"

Detective Schapiro said; "Not too much. He was in a sour mood about being questioned. I saw revenge in his eyes toward his partner. He was put in jail and awaited trial because he was deemed as a flight risk. We wanted to make sure he stuck around for the trial."

The judge interrupted and said: "Excuse me Detective Schapiro. Please do not talk about his partner. I don't want the jury influenced by the first defendant."

Detective Schapiro said: "Sorry your honor. I didn't mean to mess up the trial."

The judge said: "Because of the time we will adjourn for the day. Everybody return at 9:00 tomorrow morning. Thank you all for coming." With that the bailiff yelled "ALL RISE!!!" Everybody rose and they were escorted to the front doors of the court house. They did not take the same elevator as the previous day.

CHAPTER 24

Day 3 of the trial started with the bailiff yelling: "ALL RISE!!!" With that the judge entered right at 9:00 a.m. exactly on time. The judge said: "Good morning ladies and gentlemen of the jury. I trust you slept will last night. Jack, you may begin when ready."

Jack said: "Thank you sir. I call Moredecai to the stand." As Mordecai approached the stand he was sworn in as the witness. He then took his seat.

Jack asked; "How did you get involved in this situation?"

Mordecai said: "My partner in crime came up with it."

Jack asked: "You have heard the waitress testify that you are not a friendly person. Would you agree with that?"

Mordecai said: "No. I just stick to myself and I don't socialize with anybody."

Jack asked; "Do you have a job?"

Mordecai said: "No sir. Nobody will hire an ex con. I consider myself a drifter. I am essentially homeless because nobody will rent an apartment to me."

Jack asked; "What was your reaction to being arrested and accused of something else in the area of crime?"

Mordecai said: "I know I never kelled anyone, so I figured they will question me and apologize for interrupting my day. I fully expected to be released that day. As a criminal cops will go after a former convict if they can't find a real suspect."

Jack said: "No more questions your honor."

The judge said: "Julian, do you have any questions for this witness?"

Julian said: "I do your honor. Now Mordecai, why did you do this act?"

Mordecai said; "I tried to do something naughty just to get arrested. I can't get a job or rent an apartment. At least in jail I have a roof over my head and three square meals a day. I used my brother's name to get one apartment, but I didn't know people actually check into the information."

Julian asked: "So why did you want to go back to jail?"

Mordecai said: "In school all they taught me

was academics. They did nothing to teach me about being an adult. How to walk, how to talk proper English, how to dress etc. Because of that I couldn't get right a job interview. I had no experience with anything. I couldn't show that I did anything."

Julian asked: "Did your school make you do community service?"

Mordecai said: "No sir. I might have gotten experience if I had. All I did was go to school and come home and do homework. Nothing else."

Julian asked: "Did you like it in jail?"

Mordecai said: "Nobody likes it in jail. All they did was lock me in a cell and not teach me how to improve my life."

Julian asked: Did you talk to a psychiatrist?"

Mordecai said: "Yes. But he didn't do anything for me."

Julian asked: "Did you get any visitors in jail?"

Mordecai said: "No sir. I was locked up and forgotten about."

Julian asked: "What didn't you like about the psychiatrist?"

Mordecai said: "That idiot kept trying to get me to say everything in my life was my fault. It was the educational system's fault for not doing their job.

They should have done a better job of teaching me something."

Julian said: "So you think it is the educational system's fault for you turning to a life of crime. They are to blame for your actions."

Mordecai said: "That's right."

Julian said: "Thank you Mordecai. No more questions your honor."

The judge said: "You may step down Mordecai. Jack, call your next witness please."

Jack said: "I call Mary Kelly to the stand." As Mary approached she was sworn in as a witness. He said: "Mary, please state your occupation."

Mary said: "I am the warden in the local jail."

Jack asked: "How do you remember the defendant?"

Mary said: "I read his file yesterday. I found him to be a very uncooperative prisoner. He did not do his job or his extra work. We tried to give him homework for his GED exam, but he wouldn't do it. Miracle of miracles he passed on the first try."

Jack asked: "How did the guards treat him?"

Mary said: "They tried to treat him with respect, but he never reciprocated. The guards had to get rough with him. His biggest fight with us was the strip search. He refused to bend over and let us look up his heiney hole. That is where prisoners hide their drugs. He also would not spread his family jewels. Prisoners can tape drugs between there too."

Jack asked; "What else goes up there?"

Mary said: "Petroleum jelly. Anything that doesn't cut you. Prisoners will do anything for a trip to the hospital."

The judge interrupted and said: "Excuse me Mary. The jury will disregard that last statement. He is not on trial for his family jewels."

Mary said: "I apologize your honor. I didn't mean to mess up the trial."

Jack asked: "What do you do if a prisoner is claiming constipation?"

Mary said: "The prison doctor pokes around up there. He is given 3 drinks a day of Citrucel to soften the stool. If after five days he still hasn't moved he is given a trip to the hospital. He is handcuffed the whole time."

Jack asked: "Has there ever been an incident that required a trip to the hospital?"

Mary said: "Yes. One time only. That one swallowed kitechen utensils, but he died on the operating table. I had to stay behind and nofiy his family. They were there when he died. I allowed the family to take immediate possession of the body. I atteneded the wake and funeral."

Jack said: "Thank you Mary. No more questions your honor."

The judge said: "Julian, do you have any questions for this witness?"

Julian said: "No sir. No questions for this witness."

The judge said: "Very well. You may step down Mary."

CHAPTER 25

The judge said: "We will adjourn for the day. Tomorrow morning at 9:00 a.m. we will continue with the closing arguments. After that you will start to deliberate."

With that the bailiff yelled "ALL RISE"!!! With that everybody rose and the jury was escorted from the courtroom and out of the courthouse.

Trh next day the two lawyers met and were given the set of rules for the closing arguments. They weren't allowed to mention the name or punishment of the other defendant. Actually the lawyeres didn't know nyway, so that was no problem there. When the judge finished he bad them all a good night. He asked if there were any questions and both lawyers said: "No sir. No questions." With that they all went home for a good night's rest. Actually they didn't really sleep, they had to write their closing arguments. They had to look alive and awake by 9:00. They also had to memorize their closing arguments because reading from a piece of paper was not allowed.

CHAPTER 26

At precisely 9:00 a.m. everybody assembled in the courtroom to await the start of the day. The bailiff yelled: "ALL RISE!!" With that everybody rose and the judge entered. One juror got so used to it that that night she rose when her husband entered the room. He was so impressed he brought her flowers. She said it was force of habit from the trial.

The judge entered and said good morning to the jury. He said: "Jack, you may begin your closing arguments now."

Jack got up and said: "Thank you your honor. Ladies and gentelemen of the jury. There is no question that my client is guilty. But guilty of what? He never touched the horse. His fingerprints were not on the bridle or harness. This is Las Vegas after all. It is a little hard to walk down the stret with a horse and not be noticed. How on earth would it be possible to get a horse through swinging revolving doors through a mall no less. My client was never seen in the company of the horse. All he is guilty of is talking to someone about doing something. The last I checked that wasn't a crime. Thank you."

The judge said: "Julian, you may begin when ready."

Julian got up and said: "Thank you your honor. Ladies and gentlemen of the jury. It is no secret that my client is guilty of conspiracy to commit a felony. He talked about the crime to his co-conspirator. He is guilty, but should be found not guilty. Please allow me to explain. We have proven that the bigger problem here is not his conversation with someone, but the bigger problem is the educational system that failed to educate my client. He revealed to me that he was turned down for financial aid. He had no way of paying for college. Nobody would give him a job. Why didn't the educational system teach him how to do a job interview? My client also revealed to me that he has no health insurance. As long as he is in jail the state will pay for his medical needs. Sending him back to jail would be a blessing for him. Society is at fault for his behavior. Thank you."

The jduge said; "Ladies and gentlemen. You have heard closing arguments from both sides. This defendant is charged with conspiracy to commit a felony. A felony is stealing something that is worth more than $1,000.00. Take your time with this decision. With that the bailiff led the jury into the deliberation room. When they got in there they found a pot of coffee, a pot of hot water, cookies, and fruit. No peanuts though because the judge didn't want to risk anybody having an allergy attack. The bailiff broke the rules and said: "I am begging you to finish today. The judge's son is being circumcised tomorrow and we all want to keep him happy. Please don't tell him I said anything. All the jurors agreed to keep that part out of it. The bailiff said to send him a note that he will pass on to the judge when they finished. After an hor or so of negotiating they all agreed to a guilty verdict of conspiracy. He was ordered back to jail for life. Some people brought the argument that the educational school system was at fault. Four people thought that was a load of bologna.

Back in the court room the judge said: "Will the defendant please rise?" The defendant and his lawyer both rose in unison. The jury foreperson handed the not to the judge. The judge read it aloud and said "Guilty!!" This was no surprise to anyone. He was sentenced to life in prison without the possibility of parole. It was his third strike against society. The jduge requested that the defendant be carted off to jail immediately. He was housed in a separate unit from the normal prisoners. Lifers were housed in Unit L for lifer. He was given his usual white jump suit. He revealed to the guards that he pretended to be suicidal only so the guards would come to see him. He longed for company.

CHAPTER 28

The lawyeres were summoned to the judge's office for a dressing down scream session. Julian broke the rules given to them that he was not to bring up the co defendant. He kept apologizing up and down, but it did not good. The judge threatened to throw both lawyers in jail, but backed down on that. He just wanted to make his point clear. The judge's rules were to be followed to the letter. They were both dismissed. They stalked down the hall with their tails between their legs. The judge left the court house and went home. He had to put his anger aside for the sake of his son's brisk. He then had to clean his house from top to bottom. He wife did nothing all day. All she did was take care of the baby. An 8 day old baby sleeps all day. They started arguing about that. Then when the Rabbi showed up they both up on a brave face and smiled all night. The baby didn't sleep that night because he was probably sour in his nether regions.

CHAPTER 29

Meanwhile Mordecai's lawyer requested an appeal of the sentence. He thought it was rather harsh.

The judge said: "The appeals court is the stone building across the street. Feel free to file the papers."

He had to work within the time limit of 72 hours. The appeals court agreed to hear the case, but it was too late. Mordecai commited suicide in his jail cell by ramming his head into the stone wall. He was found the next day. He left a note that he couldn't spend the rest of his life couped up inside of four stone walls. His family took possession of the body ad he was cremated. The jail unit had a memorial service for him. Everybody liked him, but he never gave them the cance to show it. They did that for every dead lifer that came through the unit. Surprisingly Unit L was the unit of least trouble. Mary checked in on them every day. Some of these guys were used for troubled teens to change their ways. That earned them an extra hour out of their cells at the end of the day. She watched on closed circuite TV that they didn't step over the line.

Mary was shocked to learn that Mordecai actually had a family. She learned that his family lived in New York and they lost touch with him. He was always full of anger because of the nuns in the 1960s and 1970s. They did all they could to get him help, but he never accepted any help from anyone. His parents had no idea he was in jail. They just prayed that he got help and that he was safe somewhere. They saw it on the news that their son was executed. You raise your kids as best you can and hope they come back and invite you into their lives.

THE END

Stay tuned in late 2013 for my 6th novel Hostages on the subway. Thank you to all who read my books. You will not be disappointed. Here are excerpts from that book.

Excerpts from my next book
HOSTAGES ON THE SUBWAY

CHAPTER 1

On July 1st 2000 the then governor of Nevada had the budget to build the city's first subway. It was decided that it should run from the strip to downtown Las Vegas City for the commuters. It was an approximate 40 minute trip from the hospital to the strip. It was also meant to cut down the overcrowding on the buses. There was too much trouble with the tourists not knowing how much the carfare was. It also slowed down the trip to the mall. The buses were constantly late. When word came out that there will be a subway built it looked like everybody in the United States made a trip to Las Vegas. The workers had to prove they were licensed engineers. They hired current Las Vegas residents first. Because of all the applicants the lines downtown had to be organized by the cops. There was no room on the sidewalk for anybody. The applications were stopped and picked up tomorrow in the convention center inside. At least there was no traffic jam on the sidewalk anymore. After this was over the numbers came out the following month and the state of Nevada had the lowest unemployment rate in the United States.

CHAPTER 2

Detective Robert Schapiro and his wife became close friends with Ronald and Eloise Dennelly over the last 3 years. They were in the diner having breakfast before a picnic lunch at the park. Ronald and Eloise had a 2 year old daughter who was very well behaved in public. There was no screaming or throwing of food. Dectective Schapiro and his wife were the godparents of little Arlene. Robert almost missed the baptism because of his lateness. He made it barely by the skin of his teeth. Just as expected Robert got a phone call and was called to the commissioner's office about a forth coming issue. Robert was not allowed to talk about it. Arlene just liked to stare at people. In the next booth was Abraham and Adam. They were creeped out by the kid staring. Neither one of them liked kids. Especially babies her age. Babies her age had a a reputation for being sloppy. Ronald and Eloise made the mistake of planning their day with other people eavesdropping. Robert dropped money on the table to pay his half of the bill and left promptly. They decided to take the new train to the hospital and walk to the park and eat lunch.

CHAPTER 3

braham and Adam were 2 residents of the state of Nevada. They were disgusted with the whole state because they were rejected from working on the new railway. Adam told Abraham to follow him and to follow his lead. They followed Ronald and Eloise and the whole group to the first stop on the subway. They followed at a discreet distance. They sat down on a fountain and faced Ronald's back and watched for a while. Adam said: "Today we will take hostages on the subway. Nobody will get hurt, but I want revenge against the people who built the subway." They continued following the group until they reached the stop where they got on the train. It was the first stop by Bally's. They planned to take it to the last stop by the hospital. Abraham was apprehensive about taking hostage the wife of a cop, but Adam told him not to worry. They will get off if she doesn't get hurt.

Abraham asked: "How much ransome will you ask for?"

Adam said: "I don't know yet."

Abraham asked: " What if they see us and get suspicious?"

Adam said: "We are just 2 other people on the subway. As long as we don't draw attention to ourselves they have no reason to be suspicious of me or you. How many people do you see on this platform?"

Abraham said: "A lot. Maybe a hundred people."

Adam said: "What is so special about us as opposed to the other 98 people? We just look like tourists."

CHAPTER 4

Robert got a phone call while he was in a meeting with Norman, the commissioner. He apologized for the interruption.

Norman said: "Answer that Robert."

Robert picked up the phone and discovered that it was his wife. She was very upset when she talked to him. Robert said: "Honey, what is wrong? You know I can't talk to you while I am in a meeting."

His wife said: "I am sorry honey. There is a man here who says he will kill everybody on this train if you don't get down here and hire him and his friend."

Robert said: "I am here will Norman the commissioner. I will put you on speaker phone. You know I can't hire people on the spot. Get them on the phone and I will talk to them."

She did and Robert said: "Who is this?"

Adam said: "My name is Adam. I have one request. I will be hired to work for this railroad or I will kill everybody on this train. Me and my friend Abraham were rejected. We have not had any job for 2 years now and the frustration is getting to me. I can't take it anymore."

Robert said: "I will talk to the person in charge of the railroad. But you must promise me nobody will get hurt."

Adam said: "I have taken hostage the conductor. He is knocked out cold, but he will come through pretty soon. We didn't hurt him too hard."

CHAPTER 5

Norman said: "You know you can't get involved if you are in a case personally. We went over this already."

Robert said: "I know that sir. How should we handle this?"

Norman said: "Get geared up and call your team together. Everybody get dressed in full regalia and drive down to the subway. Then I will take over. Within 3 minutes everybody was on their way to the subway and awaited further instruction. The strip was cleared of everybody. Cops lined up everywhere shooing people inside. Everybody cooperated fully. Most people ran into the nearest mall. The police tape was stretched across the street. Traffic came to a standstill. The stores in the malls were over the moon with delight. The casinos were all excited because everybody went in there and people tried to figure out how to play. They made a lot of money that day. People tried to play roulette and black jack.

The casinos put on extra shows for free to entertain the masses. Some people found windows to look out on to watch the show. While half the police department was on the strip one person went on the internet to figure out who was in charge of hiring and firing of the new subway. They came up with the name Jimmy Black. Jimmy was found immediately and driven down to the scene of the crime. The expert hostage negotiator went to work trying to free the hostages. Robert's wife was pushed up front to show Robert that they weren't harmed.